U0045186

偉大　世界　自由　思想

大地

互古　　　　　　光明

愛　　　　　　　永世

自由集
The Freedom

真與美

白家華／著‧譯

要寫就寫不一樣的：
《自由集》雙語創寫

寫完了〈新的力量 The New Strength〉這一首，裡頭有這樣的句子：「₁我的航行已到達它的終點，₂我力已竭，₃而生命之舟已擱淺在岸邊。

₁My voyage has reached its end, ₂I have been exhausted, ₃and the boat of life has been stranded on the shore.」至此，有「終點」、「力竭」、「擱淺」等詞彙，我便覺得自己已經得到了「暗示」(hint)，隱射《自由集 The Freedom》在歷經 53 首的整理過程之後，已經完稿了！

凡是身爲「神秘色彩」的一位作者，其詩作之刻鑿痕跡皆已降至最低，甚至無法被察覺，遣詞造句似行雲流水之天成，且對於「自然而至」、「超乎人力」之「暗

示」是敏感的，甚至是「多疑」。所以，篇幅（53首）既已確定，那麼，便會把稿子交出去；這一本「主流外」、「雙語創作」的詩集，就能夠面世了呢！

《自由集 The Freedom》的詩歌雙語創寫，比起前兩本來，心態上是更為自在很多，也有「享受創寫過程」的愜意。這或許是因為前兩本把我想展現的都已經大部分地展現出來了吧！

而且這一本同樣被我自己視為「代表作」的、「第三本代表作」的詩集，我對於它的篇數並不怎麼要求了，落在只有 50 到 60 首之間而已，但它的「含量」包括在「藝術性」、「獨創性」、「一貫性」以及「困難度」這些方面，並不會降低，到現在已經完成了；相對於它的篇幅傾向於「薄」或「輕」，前兩本《流雲集 Drifting Clouds》跟《世界集 Worlds》是屬於「大部頭」的。

此本詩集在排版方式，與前兩本《流雲集 Drifting Clouds》、《世界集 Worlds》略有不同，不但每一首都訂有題目，且在中文部分都加入了「上標」的「句數」標示，於英文則是「下標」的，儼然是對於作品的某種要

4

求，而事實上在我這階段的風格尚未成熟的當年，我就是用這種方法來幫助自己，來看清楚我自己的詩作的贅冗或簡潔。

對「藝術」報以「忠誠」；對於「藝術」包含「文學」回報以「忠誠」，這並非從我開始的，已有若干位先賢都是這樣渡過他們的「寫作」的一生，包括歌德對於「浮士德」的慢工出細活、直到將死之年才完成它，也包括紀德在初次出版他的代表作〔地糧〕時、只印刷了 300 本、那般地敬重而不浮濫。

每望及這些位前賢戒慎的堅決姿態，便欣有慰藉與契合！

我從當初的信念包括「要寫就寫不一樣的」這一個念頭開始，直到如今有這樣稍微看得到的成果，把空泛得只是一句話的理想給落實了，這前後已經橫跨了正好三十年之久呢！還是有「使命感」的成分在；願意用自己辛苦掙得的血汗錢來出版自己辛苦寫成的詩作，就是要讓這一條風格迥異的詩歌命脈不致夭折，儘量能夠延續得久些！

我長達數十年的創作生涯，寫的作品絕大部分都是不具有參賽資格，也不適合投稿的，但在我看來卻是更為重要、更值得我去努力與奉獻的；那段漫長的日子裡，如果我有需要在物質方面求得支援，主要是來自於我劬勞的母親，也讓她吃了不少苦！

　　但很慶幸的是，我居然還來得及報答她，讓我稍微減少掉些許的虧欠感！

目　錄

自由集

自由集

自 由

　　[1]自由也在時空裡，[2]似海洋與陸地來自於您那裡；[3]它們是深廣到毫無邊際。[4]我的言詞的遠展之翼的飛翔，[5]與閃電的怒吼一般，[6]永遠無法到達您的遠方。

　　[7]被賜給光芒的金羽翅也是卓絕的，[8]且能夠飛翔得迅疾又自在；[9]光芒從它的漸滅中獲得了另一次的新生，[10]卻仍無法到達您的遠方。

　　[11]星雲也是多到不可盡數，[12]因彼此間的遙遠距離而相互倚近。[13]啊，那麼我又何須認為自己是渺小的短暫的而感到恍惶呢？[14]當我所擁有的從我這裡失去時，[15]在您那裡可以把它們再重新找回。

The Freedom

　　[1]The freedom is also in time and space [2]like the ocean and land come from thy side; [3]they are so deep and wide that they are boundless. [4]The flight of the far-spreading wings of my words [5]will never reach thy

distance ₆like the roar of lightning.

₇The golden feather wings given to the light are also unsurpassed ₈and can fly fast and freely; ₉the light gets another new life from its disappearance, ₁₀but still cannot reach thy distance.

₁₁Nebulae are too numerous to be counted, ₁₂and are close to each other because of the far distance between them. ₁₃Ah, then why should I think that I am small and short-lived and feel hesitant and panicky? ₁₄When what I have are lost from me, ₁₅they can be found again at thy side.

自 由 的 充 滿

¹我感到自由的充滿，²飛翔之族因它而得以振翅向前。

³清澈的一種流淌因它而得以遍佈在天地間，⁴也將

The Freedom

潤澤來普施，⁵使苞成花。

⁶水珠的隊伍，⁷雨的子裔，⁸離開了天上的淨居，⁹又在地上覓得了另一個居所。

¹⁰而太陽，¹¹這一盞亙古的巨大明燈，¹²仍用光與熱的禮物來祝福我們的大地。

The Fullness of Freedom

₁I feel the fullness of freedom, ₂and the flying flocks are able to flutter forward because of it.

₃A kind of clear flow can spread all over the world because of it ₄and give the moisture universally ₅to make buds turn into flowers.

₆The team of water droplets, ₇the descendants of rain, ₈leave the pure dwelling in the sky ₉and find another dwelling on the ground.

₁₀And the sun, ₁₁this huge eternal lamp, ₁₂still uses the gifts of light and heat to bless our earth.

必要的自由

[1]我尚且未能確切知曉，[2]自由來自何處，[3]但您已給了我們那必要的自由，[4]以致腳能行走而翅能飛翔！

[5]當種子變成清輕的芽，[6]它們就從地下的幽暗世界出發，[7]向地上的廣大世界去茁長。

[8]種子的心中含有無畏懼的看不見的勇氣，[9]快意地隨風遠揚，[10]萌芽於瘠土之上，[11]並用贏取到的芬芳榮譽來獻給您。

The Necessary Freedom

[1]I still do not know exactly [2]where the freedom comes from, [3]but thou hast given the necessary freedom to us [4]so that the feet can walk and wings fly!

[5]As seeds turn to fresh light buds, [6]they depart from the gloomy world underground [7]to grow toward the vast world on the ground.

[8]The hearts of the seeds contain fearless invisible

courage, ₉happily flying afar with the wind, ₁₀sprout on the barren soil, ₁₁and present thee with the honour of fragrancy which they have won.

接納

¹花朵享有自由，²那來自於您的，³在它們的盛放中，⁴但當它們枯萎而結成果實，⁵就享有另一種福分！

⁶我在生命中的所有努力，⁷似乎都是爲了這一刻而做準備，⁸就像那開了又謝了的春蕊，⁹於秋天到來時變爲成熟的果實。

¹⁰我在我生命裡所做的一切努力，¹¹都將匯合成爲甜美豐實的收穫，¹²而您會賜予我另一種榮耀，¹³以您的接納！

¹⁴當我獻出此生的甜美果實，¹⁵我將毫無遺憾了！

¹⁶我曾努力地紮根過，¹⁷也曾開花過。

Acceptance

1Flowers enjoy freedom, 2which comes from thee, 3in their full bloom, 4but when they wither into fruit, 5they enjoy another blessing!

6All my efforts in life 7seem to be the preparation for this moment, 8just like the spring flower blooms and withers 9and turns to ripe fruit when autumn comes.

10All the efforts that I have made in my life 11will converge into a sweet and fruitful harvest, 12and thou wilt give me another glory 13with thine acceptance.

14I will have no regrets 15when I give of sweet fruits of this life.

16I have strived to take root 17and have blossomed.

陽光

1陽光也有它自己的自由，2去奉獻愛的能量給世

The Freedom

界，³由天到地，⁴從山至谷。

⁵萬物都有它們自己的自由，⁶去實現心中的夙願。

⁷啊，陽光所擁有的顏色，⁸雖然只是單一的，⁹但在萬物不斷茁長的生命裡，¹⁰ 我們得以看見它的愛之奉獻的繽紛色彩！

Sunlight

₁Sunlight also has its freedom ₂to dedicate love energy to the world ₃from heaven to earth, ₄from mountain to valley.

₅All things have their own freedom ₆to achieve their long-cherished wishs.

₇O the colour that sunlight has ₈is just single, ₉but in the constantly growing life of all things ₁₀we can see the colourful colours of its love devotion!

智識之光

¹亙古的「黑暗」，²有時候會令我害怕，³也使我感到孤立，⁴但更可怕的，⁵豈不是「心靈」的「黑暗」嗎？

⁶在您自己的自由中，⁷您已點燃了「太陽」，⁸使它成為一顆銀色恆星，⁹而您也賦予「智識」以光明，¹⁰它是開放給人們去尋求的。

¹¹「智識」之光，豈曾隱滅過？¹²它總是等候在那裏，¹³等待「心靈」衝破自己「盲昧」的黑暗，¹⁴去領受它的財富。

The Light of Knowledge

[1]The ancient Darkness [2]sometimes scares me, [3]and makes me feel isolated, [4]but is the more terrible thing [5]not the Darkness of Mind?

[6]In thine own freedom, [7]thou hast ignited the Sun [8]and hast made it a silver star, [9]and thou hast endowed Knowledge with the brightness, [10]which has been open to

The Freedom

people to seek.

₁₁Has the light of Knowledge ever been extinguished?
₁₂It always waits there, ₁₃waiting for the Heart to break
through the darkness of its own Blindness ₁₄and to receive
its wealth.

純粹的光芒

¹死去後，²我與你一同散發的純粹的光芒，³及我
生命中的小哀愁，⁴將從眼前隱匿，⁵在無光的黑暗中。

⁶而我明瞭，吾愛，⁷一顆恆星於毀滅以後，⁸仍將
與它的微塵在同一個世界裡，⁹它是廣大得有一點擁擠
的！

The Pure Light

₁After death, ₂the pure light that I radiate with you
₃and the little sadness in my life ₄will disappear from sight

₅in the darkness without light.

₆But I realize, my love, ₇that a star after it dies ₈will still be with its dust in the same world, ₉which is vast enough to be a little crowded!

創造的洪流

¹您的創造的洪流汎溢整個世界；²它的「美」的涓滴注入我心，³被坦露在我的這些抒情詩裡。⁴是否我未經修飾的即興的歌唱聲，⁵讓您聽見您自己創造力的迴響呢？

⁶這生命之歌，⁷我與您合唱的，⁸必將被淹沒在世界的永久沉默中。⁹歌詞將重又保持岑寂，¹⁰ 但旋律將依然迴響在我心裡。

The Flood of Creation

₁The flood of thy creation overflows the whole world;

The Freedom

₂drips of its Beauty pour into my heart ₃to be revealed in these lyric poems of mine. ₄Do my unmodified impromptu songs allow thee ₅to hear the echo of thine own creativity?

₆This song of life, ₇which I sing with thee, ₈will surely be submerged in the eternal silence of the world. ₉Lyrics will once again maintain stillness, ₁₀but the melody will keep echoing in my heart.

開放的財富

¹那是您的沉默大地的穩重，²使我心的活潑大海得以湧現出浪花的笑容。

³您的夏陽從不炫耀他自己的強光，⁴且他無法像秋月那麼柔和。

⁵您的寒冬讓我體悟暖春的可貴；⁶炎夏使我憶起清秋之可喜。

⁷您的流星毫無畏懼地前進，⁸儘管它終將消逝，⁹

24

且夜空依舊只是默默地凝視著。

　　¹⁰ 您的星斗總是不斷地發出它們自己的光芒，¹¹不管它們是否被看到。

　　¹²您的春之晨光已經在路上召喚著我的心；¹³就讓我的希望之芽打開它的種子的殼的大門吧！

　　¹⁴而您的天空依然照常給我繁星的開放財富，¹⁵縱然在夜裡我已經持有我為自己點亮的燈的財產。

The Open Wealth

₁It is the stability of thy silent earth ₂that makes the lively sea of my heart burst into the smile of waves.

₃Thy summer sun never shows off his own glare, ₄and he cannot be as mild as the autumn moon.

₅Thy cold winter makes me realize the preciousness of the warm spring; ₆the hot summer reminds me of the loveliness of clear autumn.

₇Thy meteor advances without fear ₈even though it

will fade away, ₉and the night sky still only stares in silence.

₁₀Thy stars always glow constantly with the light of their own, ₁₁whether they are seen or not.

₁₂The morning light of thy spring has called my heart on the road; ₁₃just let the sprout of my hope open the door of the shell of its seed.

₁₄And thy sky still gives me the open wealth of numerous stars as ever ₁₅though I have held the property of my lamps lit for myself at night.

芬芳財富

¹我真正地得到你的芬芳財富的時機已過，²因為我只顧著搜集它。

³短暫的是，⁴你這盛開花朵的生命，⁵但仍然勇敢的是你展現出你自己的真與美。

⁶當你不再是正值青春盛開的一朵鮮花，⁷而是枯萎的落花，⁸就讓我依然對你說：「⁹你是如此芬芳、美麗且年輕啊！」

Wealth of Fragrance

₁The opportunity for me to truely get your wealth of fragrance has passed, ₂for I just focus on gathering it.

₃Brief is the life of you, ₄the blooming flower, ₅and still brave are you to show your truth and beauty.

₆When you are no longer a youthful, blooming and fresh flower, ₇but a withered and fallen one, ₈just let me still say to you," ₉Oh, you are so fragrant, beautiful and young!"

生命

¹生命是他的燭之燃焰，²而它的光明是被無邊際的

死之長夜黑暗籠罩著。

　³生命是在死亡陰影下的一場硬仗；⁴讓我把自己成爲像戰士一樣吧！⁵因而我並不懼怕它。

　⁶生命是您的世界裡的一座小小孤島，⁷被環繞以死亡的汪洋，⁸用深邃的曲調日以繼夜地對它低吟或高歌。

Life

₁Life is the burning flame of his candle, ₂and its light is shrouded in the boundless long night darkness of death.

₃Life is a tough battle under the shadow of death; ₄let me make myself soldierlike, ₅so I just fear not it.

₆Life is a tiny little island in thy world, ₇surrounded by the ocean of death, ₈which whispers or chants it deep tunes day and night.

生命的太陽

¹我這生命的太陽也曾經輝煌過；²現在它的青春就快要消逝了，³收斂起最後的餘光，⁴融入您那永恆冰冷的夜裡。

⁵但於死亡的清醒中，⁶讓她的心依然連繫著我的心吧，⁷因為在生之夢裡，⁸我們已經相愛過彼此了！

Sun of Life

₁This sun of my life was also once glorious; ₂now its youth is about to fade away, ₃put away the last afterglow ₄and blend in with thine eternal cold night.

₅But in the awakening of death ₆let her heart still be connected with mine, ₇for we have loved each other ₈in the dream of life.

愁 緒

¹秋氣的薄紗，²覆蓋著大地；³街景變得矇矓似夢。⁴它更輕的覆蓋是在我心頭上，⁵引起我淡淡的愁緒。

⁶這離別的愁緒流經我心，⁷且坦露成爲甜美詩歌。⁸它亦將回歸汝處而受撫平，⁹再一次地撒落成爲淅瀝秋雨，¹⁰並吹拂成爲蕭瑟冬風。

Melancholy

₁The thin veil of autumn atmosphere ₂covers the earth; ₃the street scene becomes hazy like a dream. ₄Its slighter covering is on my heart, ₅causing my faint melancholy.

₆This melancholy of parting flows through my heart, ₇and it is revealed to be sweet poems. ₈It will also return to your place, ₉once again sprinkle as the pattering autumn rain, ₁₀and blow as the bleak winter wind.

離去

¹即使我不得不離去，²星辰依然會爲你發光，³冬雨仍將化爲夏泉去斟滿你的空杯與空罐。

⁴假使該說的都已說完，⁵歌曲也已唱畢，⁶就靜靜地保持聲音的永久沉默吧！⁷啊，吾愛，⁸路過的風仍將爲你帶來花的淸香，⁹而舊路的盡處有它新徑的開端！

Leaving

₁Even if I have to leave, ₂stars will still shine for you, ₃and the winter rain will still turn into summer springs to fill your empty cup and empty pot.

₄If all that should be said have been said, ₅and songs have been sung, ₆just quietly keep the lasting silence of the sounds! ₇Ah, my love, ₈the passing wind will still bring you the fresh fragrance of flowers, ₉and the end of an old road has its beginning of a new path.

The Freedom

足跡

¹從已遭廢棄的舊址傳來了一個深沉的聲音，²也在我心中迴蕩著：「³在這裡我曾經生活過，⁴也愛過了。」

⁵你的足跡可以被消滅掉，⁶但你早已走過的事實卻無法被抹煞。

⁷當他們消滅掉留在俗世裡的你的足跡時，⁸你早已走過的事實之真實性，⁹仍然永不改變！

Footprints

₁A deep voice came from the abandoned old site, ₂and echoed in my heart," ₃Here I have ever lived ₄and loved."

₅Your footprints can be wiped out, ₆but the fact that you had walked cannot be erased.

₇When they wipe out your footprints left in the world, ₈the truth of the fact that you had walked ₉still never changes!

您 的 身 邊

¹世界必將在我眼前閉上他最後的眼睛，²星辰不再發光，³且風兒不再歌唱。

⁴我將完成此世的分階段任務，⁵連一個易逝的潰跡也未留下。

⁶我必將又回到您的身邊，⁷我的來處，⁸像雲朵完成它化爲陣雨的任務，⁹又回去妝點您的天空的鬢角。

Thy Side

₁The world will close his last eyes before my eyes, ₂stars will no longer shine, ₃and the wind will no longer sing.

₄I will complete the phased tasks of this life ₅without leaving even a transient mark.

₆I will surely return again to thy side, ₇where I come from, ₈like the cloud completes its task of turning itself into the rain shower ₉and then goes back to decorate the

The Freedom

sideburns of thy sky.

那 一 瞬 間

¹您耐心地等待過數不清的世紀，²去到達成功的那一瞬間，³使大地的汪洋與它的山脈的波浪凝固著。

⁴高空俯視著地面，⁵而地面仰望著高空。⁶天與地的這種亙古的相互凝視，⁷宛如真愛的一個不渝形式，⁸就在這愛中，⁹萬物誕生且成長。

¹⁰而我覺得星是以天為地；¹¹它們日以繼夜地成長，¹²直到開出成熟的光之花。

The Moment

₁Thou hast waited patiently for countless ages ₂to reach the moment of success ₃to make the ocean of the earth and waves of its mountains solidify.

₄The air overlooks the ground ₅and the ground looks

up at the air. 6The eternal mutual gaze of the sky and the earth 7is just like an enduring form of true love 8in which 9all beings are born and grow.

10And I think that the stars take the sky as the earth; 11they grow day and night 12until bearing mature flowers of light.

溫暖的角隅

1當我醒來時，2我伸展我的雙臂；3夜已逝。4你的太陽與我的小燈，5互相襯托著，6在它們的美之中。

7我忽然感知，8在你我之間歲月又消逝得更多了，9像不斷奔流而去的河中之水一樣，10而我在這世上又遭受到了更多必要的磨難。

11但我總不遺忘，12有一個的溫暖角隅是你永遠爲我留著的，13就在你身旁。

14黑雲化成驟雨去加入了河流，15這只是一時的，16

The Freedom

並非永久的；¹⁷啊，那些雨水又將經由河流再回到天空裡，¹⁸去成爲雲朶！

A Warm Corner

₁As I wake up, ₂I stretch my arms; ₃the night is gone. ₄Your sun and my eaves lamp ₅set off each other ₆in their beauty.

₇ I suddenly feel that ₈much more time between you and me has passed ₉like the water in rivers that constantly runs away, ₁₀and I have suffered more necessary hardships in the world again.

₁₁But I never forget that ₁₂there is a warm corner that you always keep for me, ₁₃just beside you.

₁₄It is just temporary ₁₅but not long-lasting ₁₆that black clouds dissolve into sudden rains to join rivers; ₁₇O those rain waters will get back to the sky through rivers ₁₈to become clouds again!

偉 大

¹您的「偉大」是恆以「卑微」爲基礎的。

²當我登上了那一座孤峰之頂時，³我清楚地發現到，⁴那裡所有的路都引向低處。

⁵「偉大」從來都不離棄他自己的「卑微」而成就了他自己。

⁶您是如此偉大，⁷以致我不知該如何向您致敬。

⁸因此我的燈雖然是小的，⁹我仍願把它加入您的銀河中，¹⁰去漂流在您的光的無盡大海裡。

Greatness

₁Thy Greatness is constantly based on Humbleness.

₂When I reached that isolated mountain peak, ₃I clearly found that ₄all the roads there led to low places.

₅Great never forsakes his own Humbleness and makes himself.

₆Thou art so great ₇that I know not how to pay tribute

The Freedom

to thee.

8Therefore though my lamp is small, 9I would like to
add it to thy galaxy 10to drift in the endless sea of thy
light.

謙卑的偉大

1當她出現來走向他，2像一個實現的夢想，3只有
他知道他自己是愛她的，4她卻渾然不知曉。

5他主動地把自己縮到很小，6讓出道路來給她行
走，7給她最大的路的自由；8他想，對她不必然一定要
擁有。

9就在這傍晚時分，10 他獨坐在自己回想的寧靜
中，11感覺到在愛的國度裡的謙卑的偉大，12與損失之
獲得。

The Greatness of Humility

1When she appeared to come to him 2like a realized dream, 3only he knew that he himself loved her, 4but she knew not at all.

5He took the initiative to shrink himself to a very small size, 6gave way to her to walk 7and gave her the greatest freedom of road; 8she thought that he did not necessarily have to own her.

9Just in the evening 10he sat alone in the peace of his own thoughts, 11feeling the the greatness of humility in the kingdom of love, 12and the loss of gain.

偉大的盛會

1這是個偉大的盛會；2啊，這裡生命的隊伍是浩浩蕩蕩的，3而我是何其榮幸，4也被給予一個位子來出席。

The Freedom

⁵縱然我所佔有的角落只是這麼小的，⁶也是如此偏僻的，⁷這對我已是一種天賜宏福了，⁸遑論我已經簽下了我自己的名字，⁹獻上了我的歌唱，¹⁰並且認識了你。

A Great Grand Meeting

₁This is a great grand meeting; ₂ah, the teams of life here are mighty, ₃and how honoured I am ₄to be also given a seat to attend.

₅Even though the corner that I occupy is only so small ₆and so remote, ₇it has been a great blessing from god to me, ₈not to mention that I have signed my own name, ₉have dedicated my singing, ₁₀and have known you already.

迎接

¹我已經完成的，²都是微小的事；³我的光陰將會被用罄，⁴但我不必為此感嘆，⁵因為一切都在您的掌握之中。

⁶在未來當我脫掉這一件夠舊的血肉之軀的外衣時，⁷我將如一位新生嬰兒般地赤裸無名，⁸而您的世界將以它的嶄新面目來迎接我。

Greeting

₁What I have done ₂are all small things; ₃my time will be used up, ₄but I have not to sigh for it ₅cause everything is under thy control.

₆In the future when I take off this coat of flesh which is old enough, ₇I will be naked and nameless like a newborn baby, ₈and thy world will greet me with its brand new features.

The Freedom

我的份兒

1由時間之槌所敲打出的我的生命之鼓的聲音，2只是零碎的，3但苦難的主旋律把它們織成一支悅耳的曲子。

4而當我完成我的份兒，5我就要交出我手中的工具。6您將把它交給另一位歌者，7來演奏他的旋律，8在我離去後的安靜中。

My Part

1The sounds of the drum of my life made by the hammer of time 2were only fragmentary, 3but the main melody of suffering wove them into a sweet tune.

4And when I have done my part, 5I will hand over the tool in my hands. 6Thou wilt give it to another singer, 7who will play his melody 8in the silence after I leave.

成全

¹我不只是一顆亮麗的星，²正如她不只是一朵芬芳的花，³因爲我獻出我的光與熱之財富給世界；⁴而你不只是廣大的天空，⁵因爲你默默地成全了我們。

⁶在光明中，⁷我簡陋瓦屋裡的一切是我自己的；⁸但當我點著的燈息滅了，⁹我發覺我的瓦屋是跟您的黑夜合一。

Completing

₁I am more than just a brilliant star ₂just as she is more than just a fragrant flower, ₃for I dedicate the wealth of my light and heat to the world; ₄and you are more than just the vast sky, ₅for you complete us silently.

₆In the light ₇everything in my poor tile house is my own; ₈but when the lamp which I light goes out, ₉I find that my tile house is the one with thy dark night.

The Freedom

允許

[1]世界之球的旋轉，[2]是快速並瞬息萬變的，[3]但做為球心的你的心，[4]卻是必要地靜寂不動。

[5]夏花被允許去成為秋果，[6]而秋果成為春芽。

[7]且讓我們所失去的一切東西，[8]都被您妥善地保存著，[9]如同您藏放銀河的珠鏈，[10] 在天空的永恆寶盒中。

Allowing

[1]The spin of the sphere of the world [2]is rapid and changes rapidly, [3]but as the center of the sphere, [4]your mind is necessarily silent and still.

[5]Summer flowers are allowed to turn to autumn fruits, [6]and autumn fruits turn to spring buds.

[7]Just let all things that we have lost [8]be properly kept by thee [9]as thou hidest the bead chains of galaxies [10]in the eternal treasure box of the sky.

愛的溫暖

¹儘管她的明眸是美麗似秋湖，²她的內心仍不失卻其深沉，³那有如夏季晴空的。

⁴我覺得她的愛的溫暖常與陽光齊來，⁵所以我認為她的心靈是跟星辰永遠同輝。

⁶她用她那太陽般的誠摯燦爛的笑容來善待我；⁷就讓我把我這陰影般的憂鬱面紗卸去吧！

The Warmth of Love

₁Though her bright eyes are beautiful like the autumn lake, ₂her heart still loses not its deepness, ₃which is like that of the clear summer sky.

₄I feel like the warmth of her love is always coming with the sunlight ₅so I think that her heart is forever shining with the star.

₆She treats me kindly with her sun-like, sincere and brilliant smile; ₇just let me remove my shadow-like veil of

The Freedom

melancholy!

廣 闊

¹積雲再怎麼厚，²也都能夠舒展且隱匿。³天空的胸懷是夠廣闊的。

⁴閃電的大笑之音總是自行消失。⁵天空必要的沉默是永久的。

⁶在夜空深處，⁷藏著一句靜默的話；⁸於他亙古深邃的心裡，⁹有一切聲音的回響，¹⁰而且他承載著我的生，¹¹還有我的死。

¹²他，永恆的，¹³永不厭惡那些短暫的喧囂音樂，¹⁴但他更愛他自己靜默的無聲之歌。

Broadness

₁No matter how thick the cumulus clouds are, ₂they all can stretch and disappear. ₃The mind of the sky is broad enough.

₄The big laughters of lightning always disappear automatically. ₅The necessary silence of the sky is permanent.

₆In the depths of the night sky ₇there is a silent sentence hidden; ₈in his deep and eternal heart ₉there are echoes of all sounds, ₁₀and he carries my life ₁₁and my death.

₁₂He, the eternal, ₁₃never hates those noisy short-lived music, ₁₄but he loves much more his own silent soundless song.

單純

¹假使我的生命，²只是蒼白如根，³就讓我別嫉妒你的存在，⁴那美麗似花的！

⁵就讓我的生命以牠自己的「單純」爲歸宿吧，⁶似陽

The Freedom

光涵容了一切色彩而變得淨白，⁷並顯出種種事物來！

⁸而你的生命也有牠自己的價值，⁹儘管牠的存在於成形之後即被吹散，¹⁰只留下短暫可見的痕跡。

Simplicity

₁If my life is only pale ₂as the root, ₃just let me not be jealous of your existence, ₄which is beautiful like the flower.

₅Just let my life take its own Simplicity as its home ₆like the sunshine contains all colors to become pure and white ₇and to show all kinds of things!

₈And your life also has its own value ₉though its existence is suddenly blown off after being formed, ₁₀leaving only a short-lived visible trace.

思 想

[1]我的思想的小水珠，[2]已匯入您的思想的無盡汪洋裡。[3]因此它將不再會乾涸了！

[4]而且所幸的是，[5]我生命的卑微歌詞，[6]仍與您的永恆旋律在共舞著；[7]且讓我唱完它；[8]莫讓它戛然而止吧！

Thought

[1]The little droplet of my thought [2]has merged into the endless ocean of thy thought. [3]Therefore it will not dry up anymore.

[4]And it is fortunate [5]that the humble lyrics of my life [6]are still dancing with thine eternal melody; [7]just let me finish singing it; [8]let it not stop abruptly!

The Freedom

一念

¹且讓我的一念越過這一座天空之屋的外面的世界之屋，²它用星河裝飾，³以雲海爲簾，⁴去會見他，⁵那永恆的一位！

⁶他將藉由我的生命，⁷這原本是一個脆薄之物，⁸演奏出更美妙的樂曲，⁹因爲它已被這塵世裡的苦難賦予了更多價值。

One Thought

₁Just let one thought of mine pass through the house of the world, ₂whose decors are made with galaxies and with curtains of the seas of clouds, ₃outside this house of the sky ₄to meet him, ₅the eternal one!

₆He wilt play more wonderful music ₇by my life, ₈which was originally a fragile and thin thing, ₉for it has been given more value by the suffering in this earthly world.

平靜

¹我何必把自己排除在外，²何必那樣迂蠢地遠離著，³或太畏怯以致無法承受愛的甜美負擔呢？

⁴其實在你深情的天地中我無處遁逃，⁵因為你總是帶來了平靜，⁶到你所到之處，⁷也把它留給你自己，⁸儘管你的每一顰蹙或莞爾，⁹都能夠移轉我的心緒，¹⁰和引發我的歡笑或憂愁。

Peace

₁Why should I exclude myself, ₂be so silly to stay away ₃or be too timid to bear the sweet burden of love?

₄In fact I have nowhere to escape in the world of your deep affection, ₅for you always bring the peace ₆to the places that you reach ₇and leave it to yourself ₈even though your every frown or smile ₉can shift my mood ₁₀and cause my laughter or sorrow.

The Freedom

目光

¹世界在我眼中，²縮小到只剩她一人，³卻又浩瀚無比，⁴因爲我的目光與她的目光相接，⁵且我和她心心相映。

⁶大影子形成黑夜，⁷來覆蓋我的睡眠，⁸而這些小的是由地上青草所成，⁹來撫慰我的心。

¹⁰但除非我真的瞭解她存在的價值，¹¹否則我將無法明白那屬於我自己的。

Eyes

₁The world shrinks to her alone ₂in my eyes, ₃yet it is incomparably vast, ₄for my eyes and her eyes meet each other, ₅and my heart is linked together with hers.

₆The big shadow forms the dark night ₇to cover my sleep, ₈and these small ones are formed by green grasses on the ground ₉to soothe my heart.

₁₀But unless I really understand the value of her

existence, ₁₁I will not realize that which belongs to me.

奮鬥的足跡

¹我奮鬥的足跡，²既無需在意這個世界是否會記住它們，³也無需證明我的腳早已走過了。

⁴讓「犧牲」因爲不謀求回報而成爲牠自己吧！

⁵於成長時，且把根紮入深處，⁶去成爲穩固的；⁷豐收時獻出甜美果實，⁸由苦澀所成的。

⁹而讓我的心永遠保有牠自己的澄淨，¹⁰以致牠可以將您的愛發揚光大！

Footprints of Struggle

₁The footprints of my struggle ₂need neither to care if this world will bear them in mind ₃nor to prove that my feet had traveled.

₄Let Sacrifice become itself for seeking no returns.

The Freedom

5When growing, just pierce roots into the depths 6to become stable; 7when harvesting, offer sweet fruits 8of bitterness.

9And let my heart always keep its own purity 10so that it can carry thy love forward!

歲月的光輝

1因為我們共同經歷過那些歲月，2它們的光輝愈增，3似昨晚短暫交會的月與雲，4對於天空所做的那樣。

5倘若從此我是孑然一身的，6像你一樣，7何不接受它呢？8我知道我們的形象的光芒已經永遠留在彼此的心裡。

The Brilliance of Years

1Because we have gone through those years together,

₂their brilliance has been increased, ₃just like what the moon did to the sky last night ₄when they met briefly.

₅If I am alone from now on ₆like you are, ₇why not accept it? ₈I know that the light of our images has remained in each other's hearts forever.

自身的美麗

¹雲族也有它們自身的彩衣，²有時閃亮似金縷，³不僅妝扮了它們自己，⁴還綴飾了天空。

⁵儘管屬於它們的生命常被認爲是小的，⁶或常被輕忽，⁷它們的存在依然有它自身的美麗。⁸啊，它們常捕捉到多彩四溢的光芒之投影，⁹並織入它們自己素樸無華的鱗衣中！

Own Beauty

₁The cloud family also have their own colourful

coats, ₂sometimes shining like gold threads, ₃that not only dress themselves ₄but also decorate the sky.

₅Though the life belonged to them is often considered to be small ₆or is often neglected, ₇their existence still has its own beauty. ₈Ah, they often capture the projections of colorful overflowing light ₉and weave them into their own unadorned scale clothes!

不變的慈愛

¹今午太陽依然用強光充塞天地中；²孩童們玩興正酣，³把空地當成遊樂場，⁴歡快地追逐；⁵一種單純的旋律飄蕩在群樹交錯的枝葉間。

⁶而昨晚無雨，⁷亦無撼動竹莖之狂風；⁸在黃昏過後，⁹在白天與大家一同工作以後，¹⁰ 我獨自走完歸途，¹¹惟見一枚孤月在卷雲後方靜靜地陪伴著我。

¹²我不知道您已來過多久了。¹³您點亮小燈留在那

裡爲著我，¹⁴於那一趟疲憊行程的盡處。¹⁵它成爲不變慈愛的印記，¹⁶成爲黑暗的頑敵。¹⁷它的亮光延伸著，¹⁸引領我進入屋內，¹⁹進入那溫暖的世界。

Unchanging Love

₁This noon the sun still fills the world with the strong light; ₂the children play happily, ₃use the open space as a playground, ₄and chase cheerfully; ₅a simple melody floats between staggered branches of trees.

₆And last night there was no rain, ₇nor the fierce wind that shook bamboo stems; ₈after dusk, ₉after working with everyone in the daytime, ₁₀I finished my way home alone ₁₁and I only saw a lonely moon quietly accompanying me behind cirrus clouds.

₁₂I did not know how long thou hadst come. ₁₃Thou lit the little lamp and left it there for me ₁₄at the end of the tiring journey. ₁₅It became the mark of thine unchanging love ₁₆and became the enemy of darkness. ₁₇Its light extended, ₁₈leading me into the house, ₁₉into the warm world.

永世之旅

¹當我初次遇見你，²我對你的認識，³如膚之淺；⁴更深刻以後，⁵漸漸地似海之厚。

⁶儘管世界必將再一次地，⁷從我眼前淡沒，⁸就讓我帶著我們共有的相聚印記，⁹踏上未完成的永世之旅！

Journey of Eternity

₁When I first met you, ₂my understanding of you ₃was as shallow as the skin; ₄after it becomes deeper, ₅it is as thick as the sea step by step.

₆Though the world will once again ₇fade out from my

eyes, ₈just let me take the common mark of our gathering ₉and embark on the unfinished journey of eternity.

新的力量

¹我的航行已到達它的終點，²我力已竭，³而生命之舟已擱淺在岸邊。

⁴光明從我眼前隱匿；⁵無邊的黑暗之覆蓋籠罩著我。

⁶但我發現，⁷新的力量就從那裡生起！⁸當海浪跌落到它自己的最低處，⁹它就從那裡再躍起，¹⁰ 而且又向前跨出一步了！

The New Strength

₁My voyage has reached its end, ₂I have been exhausted, ₃and the boat of life has been stranded on the shore.

自由集

4The light hides from my eyes; 5the shroud of boundless darkness covers me.

6But I find that 7the new strength just arises therefrom! 8When the wave sinks to its own lowest point, 9it rises again 10and takes another step forward!

記 得

1在明亮中，2當我看著你那燦爛之美時，3我仍記得在黑暗裡你的柔和。

4我的心的漂鳥，5嚮往它生命中的自由，6而你的心的世界啊，7不僅有它遨遊的天空，8還有它棲息的溫暖窩巢！

9這窩巢是小而簡的，10 我心之漂鳥卻喜歡來它裡面斂翅棲息，11只因它是在你心的無垠大地上。

Remembering

As I looked at your brilliant beauty in the light, I still remembered your softness in the dark.

The drifting bird of my heart yearns for freedom in its life, and the world of your heart, ah, has not only the sky where it travels but also the warm nest where it rests!

This nest is small and simple, but the stray bird of my heart likes coming to fold wings to roost in it, just for it is on the boundless earth of your heart.

珍惜

讓花朵的這些種籽，成爲我心的帆船吧，並用風的力量，航行於半空中的無海之海上！

在享有它們的果實的甜美時，莫忘記犧牲掉它們自己的花朵的芬芳啊！

而在珍惜一座湖的時候，讓我也同時珍惜做爲它

The Freedom

的源頭的河流！

Cherishing

₁Let these seeds of flowers ₂be sailboats of my heart ₃and use the power of the wind ₄to sail on the sealess sea in mid air.

₅When enjoying the sweetness of their fruit, ₆forget not the fragrance of flowers that sacrifice themself.

₇And when cherishing a lake, ₈let me also cherish the river which is its source.

迴響

¹我們已離開那裡多年了，²各自帶走些許回憶，³成爲昨日的廻響。

⁴新人們就像我們以前那般，⁵相繼地來了又去了；⁶那些情景璀璨如那裡的夏季天空裡的浮雲。

⁷曾經你彈奏你的曲調，⁸加深我唱的歌的意義。⁹我們的曲子的旋律悠揚，¹⁰與溪谷裡的水聲，¹¹還有林子裡的風聲，¹²一同廻響。

Echoes

₁We have left there for many years, ₂and each of us has taken away some memories, ₃which become the echoes of yesterday.

₄The newcomers come and go one after another ₅just like we used to do; ₆those scenes are as bright as floating clouds in the summer sky there.

₇You once played your tune ₈to deepen the meaning of the song which I sang. ₉Our music was melodious, ₁₀echoing together ₁₁with the sound of stream water in the valley ₁₂and the sound of wind in the forest.

The Freedom

功課

¹每一次的日常經驗，²或許都小如水滴；³但在穩固的心之大地上，⁴當它們累積起來，⁵卻能夠成爲智慧的大海。

⁶從我的苦難，⁷我已學得了初階的功課，⁸像幼兒屢經跌倒而學會了行走。

⁹我已更加懂得如何防止摔倒，¹⁰ 在許多條道路上；¹¹就讓我學習更高深的課題吧！¹²我將能夠奔跑與跳躍。

Lessons

₁Every daily experience ₂may be as small as a water drop, ₃but when they accumulate ₄on the earth of a stable heart, ₅they can be a sea of wisdom.

₆I have learned the basic lessons ₇from my sufferings ₈like a child has repeatedly fallen and then has learned to walk.

9I have known how to prevent falls 10on many roads; 11let me learn more advanced topics! 12I will be able to run and jump.

安逸

1在那段年月裡，2我過得安逸，3幾度以為那就是我生命的全部，4於是您含著寬容之淚，5把苦痛帶進了我的生命的中央，6也進入了我心裡。

7我就像一個在不適宜時刻打盹的小孩，8被您含著淚打醒；9我在一個舒適的角落中清醒過來，10遍嘗了苦痛，11而進入了歡樂的核心。

Ease

1In those days 2I lived easily, 3and several times I thought that it was all of my life, 4so thou with tears of mercy 5broughtest the pain into the center of my life 6and

The Freedom

into my heart.

7I was like a child who took a nap at an inappropriate time, 8beaten awake by thee with tears in thine eyes; 9I woke up in a comfortable corner, 10tasted the pain over and over, 11and entered the core of joy.

鐐銬

1當你的欲望成爲一種鐐銬，2首先禁錮的不就是你自己嗎？3啊，可憐的你，4被束縛在你自己之中，5沒法子脫逃呢！

6當你朽去時，7你仍只能化爲塵土，8去被那永遠不鏽不蝕的另一種鐐銬給禁錮住，9即使你曾經是那麼威武的。

Shackle

1When your desire becomes a kind of shackle , 2is it

not you yourself who is the first to be imprisoned? 3Ah, poor you, 4trapped in yourself, 5have no way to escape!

6When you rot, 7you can still only turn into dust 8to be confined to another kind of shackle that will never rust and decay 9even though you were once so mighty.

掠 奪

1當他們在抵達他們的目的地時，2高聲歡呼。

3但被他們的車輪輾過的路的痛苦，4卻受到遺忘。

5「我們想要進去你的住屋，6去虔敬地禮拜你的神。」7他們溫和地說，8但他們卻不得其門而入。

9然後他們繞過我的住屋，10 去掠奪那神廟的供品。

Looting

1They cheered loudly 2when arriving at their

destination.

₃But the pain of the road that was run by their wheels ₄was forgotten.

₅" We would like to get into your house ₆to worship your god sincerely," ₇they said softly, ₈but they could not find the door to go through.

₉Then they bypassed my house ₁₀and looted the offerings of the temple.

穩靜

¹年少時，²我的生命因成長而喧躁，³如芽之所爲。

⁴現在我只願穩靜似果，⁵默默地飽含著成熟的甜美；⁶彼時的芬芳已杳，⁷而色彩也已褪去了。

⁸且我的心絃原本是不夠緊繃的，⁹但您給予它們以必要的痛苦扭絞，¹⁰來調整它們；¹¹那就是爲什麼，¹² 它們現在能夠奉獻出更優美的音樂給世界了。

Steady and Quiet

₁When I was young, ₂my life was noisy and restless from growing ₃like a bud.

₄Now I just want to be steady and quiet like a fruit, ₅silently full of the sweetness of ripeness; ₆the fragrance of that time has gone away ₇and colours have faded.

₈And my heartstrings were originally not tight enough, ₉but thou gavest them the necessary painful twists ₁₀to adjust them; ₁₁that is why ₁₂they are now able to dedicate the more beautiful music to the world.

痕跡

₁你是像那曠野之風，₂疾來又速去；₃當你在我的生命裡進出，₄即使我想留你也留不住。

₅他是那高空裡的奔雷，₆集華美色彩於一身，₇也把夜的黑暗撕成繽紛碎片；₈唉，雖然他憤怒的叫嚷聲

The Freedom

是最響亮的，9在我心的天空裡依然未留下任何痕跡！

Trace

1You are like the wind in the wilderness, 2coming and going quickly; 3when you get in and out of my life, 4I am unable to keep you even though I want to.

5He is the thunder high up in the sky 6with gorgeous colours all in one, 7and tears the darkness of night into colourful pieces; 8alas, though his angry shout is the loudest, 9it still leaves not a trace in the sky of my heart!

似曾相識

1此世之後，2我將有「似曾相識」之感，3當我再遇見你，4因為你曾漂泊著進入我的生命中，5並帶給我歡樂與哀傷。

6來世我將不把我的心交給你的心；7且讓我只是你

園子裡未被命名的一朵新花，⁸以無私之愛的芳香去充滿你的清晨！

Deja Vu

₁After this life, ₂I will have a feeling of Deja Vu ₃as I meet you again, ₄because you ever wandered and came into my life, ₅and brought me joy and sadness.

₆Next life I will not give my heart to yours; ₇let me be just a new flower that has not been named in your garden, ₈and fill your early morning with the fragrance of selfless love.

你的心的自由

¹這降雨預示你即將來臨。

²風暴隨你而至，³在虛空裡快意馳騁，⁴因為你分享給我們你的心的自由。

The Freedom

⁵但當你離去時，⁶天空又轉為晴朗；⁷騎乘著自己的雲朵們已經遠去了，⁸而你分享給我們的你心中的那自由，⁹仍然遍布整個世界。

The Freedom of Your Heart

₁This rainfall presages your coming.

₂The storm comes with you, ₃running cheerfully in the void, ₄for you share with us the freedom of your heart.

₅But when you leave, ₆the sky turns clear again; ₇clouds that ride themslves have gone away, ₈and the freedom that you have shared with us ₉still spreads throughout the world.

我生命的小屋

₁卽使我打開我自己心的大門，₂去走向外面的世界，₃寒流仍會遠去，₄把冷風由地上帶走。

　⁵即使泉水帶來了曾經融合於遠古汪洋的清涼記憶，⁶我仍覺得我永遠無法留住什麼，⁷在我生命的小屋裡，⁸因為前門總是開著的，⁹而後門也從未被鎖上。

The Little House of My Life

₁Though I open the door of my own heart ₂to go toward the world outside, ₃the cold current will still go away, ₄taking the cold wind from the ground.

₅Though spring water brings the cool memory of ever merging into the ancient ocean, ₆I still feel that I cannot ever keep anything ₇in the little house of my life, ₈for the front door is always open ₉and the back door is never locked.

深沉平靜

　¹即使雷霆仍在怒吼，²而濃重層疊的烏雲佔領了半

The Freedom

邊天，³這湖泊，⁴啊，這心靈之湖，⁵依然已經重新恢復它原有的深沉平靜了——

　　⁶因為再一次地，⁷它已經讓風又吹過，⁸讓雨打過，⁹也讓波瀾盪漾過。

Deep Peace

₁Even though the thunder is still roaring ₂and the thick layers of dark clouds are still occupying half of the sky, ₃this lake, ₄ah, this lake of the soul, ₅has still restored its original deep peace again--

₆For once again ₇it lets the wind blow over, ₈lets the rain strike, ₉and lets the waves ripple.

離別的時刻

　　¹假使離別總是必然的，²就讓我們珍惜眼前的相聚吧！³當風吹過的時候，⁴樹就與它合唱那和鳴的歌。

⁵假使離別的時刻已然來到，⁶就熄滅掉聚晤暢談的燈火吧，⁷像風吹向遠方，⁸而樹恢復了平靜！

The Time of Parting

₁If parting is always inevitable, ₂just let us cherish the present reunion! ₃When the wind blows over, ₄the tree sings in harmony with it.

₅If the time of parting has come, ₆just turn off the lights of meeting and chatting ₇like the wind blows away into the distance ₈and trees calm down again!

隱秘的語言

¹被這夜的幽暗隔絕的我們的屋子，²是靜默的，³但它們的燈火，⁴卻以一種溫暖、明亮及隱秘的語言在交談。

⁵而花朵把泥土千萬年的沉默語言，⁶轉化成為屬於

The Freedom

它們自己一時喧鬧的。

　　7而我將編織文字的絲網，8去捕捉一些縈飛不去的東西，9但讓我自己先不被黏縛住吧！

A Secret Language

　　1Our houses isolated by this gloom of night 2are silent, 3but their lights 4talk by a warm, bright and secret language.

　　5And flowers transform the silent language of the mud for thousands of years 6into a temporarily noisy one of their own.

　　7And I shall weave the web of the text 8to catch some lingering things, 9but let myself not be stuck first!

NOTE

NOTE

國家圖書館出版品預行編目資料

自由集 The Freedom／白家華著. ─初版.─臺
中市：白象文化事業有限公司，2022.8
　　　面；　公分
中英對照
ISBN 978-626-7151-34-1（平裝）

863.51　　　　　　　　　　　111008318

自由集 The Freedom

作　　　者　白家華
校　　　對　白家華
發 行 人　張輝潭
出版發行　白象文化事業有限公司
　　　　　412台中市大里區科技路1號8樓之2（台中軟體園區）
　　　　　出版專線：（04）2496-5995　　傳真：（04）2496-9901
　　　　　401台中市東區和平街228巷44號（經銷部）
　　　　　購書專線：（04）2220-8589　　傳真：（04）2220-8505
專案主編　林榮威
出版編印　林榮威、陳逸儒、黃麗穎、水邊、陳媁婷、李婕
設計創意　張禮南、何佳諠
經紀企劃　張輝潭、徐錦淳、廖書湘
經銷推廣　李莉吟、莊博亞、劉育姍、林政泓
行銷宣傳　黃姿虹、沈若瑜
營運管理　林金郎、曾千熏
印　　　刷　百通科技股份有限公司
初版一刷　2022 年 8 月
定　　　價　180 元

白象文化　印書小舖　出版・經銷・宣傳・設計
www.ElephantWhite.com.tw　自費出版的領導者　購書 白象文化生活館